The Toady
and
Dr. Miracle

Mary Blount Christian

Pictures by Ib Ohlsson

Ready-to-Read

Aladdin Books
Macmillan Publishing Company
New York

Collier Macmillan Publishers
London

AUTHOR'S NOTE

A "toady," or "toad eater," was an assistant to the charlatans who roamed the countryside in old England and in pioneer America, tricking people out of their money with phony cures.

Text copyright © 1985 by Mary Blount Christian
Illustrations copyright © 1985 by Ib Ohlsson
All rights reserved. No part of this book may be reproduced or transmitted in any form or by any means, electronic or mechanical, including photocopying, recording, or by any information storage and retrieval system, without permission in writing from the Publisher.

Aladdin Books
Macmillan Publishing Company
866 Third Avenue, New York, NY 10022
Collier Macmillan Canada, Inc.

First Aladdin Books edition 1987
Printed in the United States of America

A hardcover edition of *The Toady and Dr. Miracle* is available from Macmillan Publishing Company.

10 9 8 7 6 5 4 3 2 1

LIBRARY OF CONGRESS CATALOGING-IN-PUBLICATION DATA
Christian, Mary Blount.   The toady and Dr. Miracle.
Summary: Dr. Miracle comes to a small town to sell his cure-all and enlists a young boy to be his toady, or assistant.
[1. Medicine shows—Fiction] I. Ohlsson, Ib, date. ill. II. Title.
[PZ7.C4528To 1987]   [E]   86-22225   ISBN 0-689-71124-7 (pbk.)

To my husband, Chris,
with love
—M.B.C.

To Torben
—I.O.

Luther swung
on his front gate.
He chewed a piece of straw.
He watched a cloud of dust
rise from the road.

5

A wagon
broke through the cloud.
The sound of bells floated
on the hot breeze.

The wagon came closer.
Luther saw brass bells
tied to the horses.

"Whoa!" the driver yelled.
"Is this the road to town, boy?"
His long black mustache jumped
like a caterpillar with hiccups.

Luther's mouth opened in surprise.

The straw fell out.

Any fool could see

it was the only road there.

"Yup," he said.

There was a sign on the wagon.

Luther sounded out the words.

"Doctor Miracle's Cure-All,"

he said.

"Come here, boy,"
Dr. Miracle said.
"Are you smart?"

Luther moved closer.
"Sometimes," he said.
"Miss Primm, my teacher,
says I could be smarter
if I tried."

12

"How would you like to earn an Indian-head nickel?" Dr. Miracle asked.

Luther's eyes opened wide. "A whole nickel?"

"I need myself a toady,"
Dr. Miracle said.

Luther scratched his head.
"Can't find toads now,"
he said. "It's too dry out."

Dr. Miracle threw back his head.

He laughed.

"I don't want you
to *catch* a toad, boy.
I want you to *be* a toady.
Be in town at sundown."

15

Dr. Miracle

handed Luther a paper.

"Tack this to your fence, boy."

Then he yelled, "Giddap!"

16

The wagon rolled forward.
The bottles rattled and
the bells tinkled.
Soon the wagon was gone.

Luther stared at the paper:

DOCTOR MIRACLE'S
CURE-ALL
GOOD FOR WHAT AILS YOU
HEADACHES
TOOTHACHES
STOMACHACHES
AND MORE

Luther was not sure
what a toady was.
But he wanted that nickel.
Right before sundown,
he walked into town.

Dr. Miracle's wagon
was tied to a hitching post.
The side was open
to make a stage.

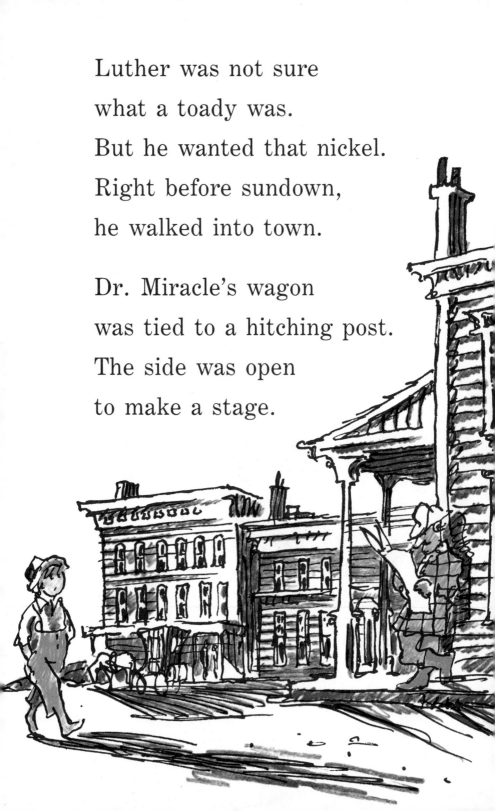

Luther peeked in.
Suddenly Dr. Miracle
pulled him inside.
"Beat this drum
to call the crowd,"
Dr. Miracle told Luther.

Luther beat the drum.

Boom! BOOM! BOOOOOM!

It sounded like thunder.

The crowd gathered.

Luther's teacher, Miss Primm, came.

His mother came, too.

Even the sheriff came.

23

Dr. Miracle
roared at the crowd.
The windows rattled.
"Do you ache, friends?
Does plowing make you tired?"
Some of the people nodded.

Dr. Miracle
held up a bottle.
"This will cure what ails you.
It's the miracle of today."

25

He put his hand
on Luther's shoulder.
"This brave lad
is from your own town,"
Dr. Miracle cried.

Luther frowned.
He did not like
being called brave.
Maybe that meant
Dr. Miracle wanted him
to do something
he did not want to do.
He tried to back away.
But Dr. Miracle would not let go.
"I'll make it two nickels, boy,"
he whispered.

"That boy is not sick!"
one man shouted.
"What are you going to cure him of?
Being dumb?"
The crowd laughed.

Dr. Miracle raised his hand
to quiet the people.
"As a matter of fact, friend,
it *can* cure dumbness.
But that is not what
I'm curing now.
Of course this boy is not sick.
But he will be!"

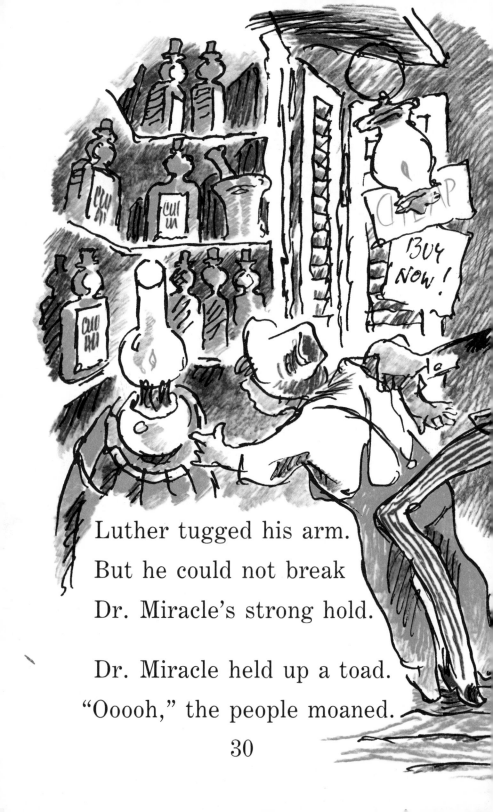

Luther tugged his arm.
But he could not break
Dr. Miracle's strong hold.

Dr. Miracle held up a toad.
"Ooooh," the people moaned.

"You know toads are poison!"
Dr. Miracle yelled. "But
this brave lad will
swallow this toad. And
Doctor Miracle's Cure-All
will save him from death!"

31

Luther tried to wiggle free.

"Stand still, boy.

This is not going to hurt!"

Dr. Miracle leaned closer.

He whispered,

"When I tell you to,

shove this toad down your shirt.

Just act as if you were swallowing."

Dr. Miracle smiled at the crowd.

"Here, boy. Now swallow!"

he said.

Luther threw back his head.

He opened his mouth wide.

He dropped the toad

head first down his shirt.

Several ladies screamed.

Miss Primm fanned herself

with her lace hanky.

"Now act sick,"

Dr. Miracle told him.

Luther crossed his eyes.
He stuck out his tongue
and grabbed his throat.
"Arrrrrrg! Aaaaaarg!"
he yelled.
He coughed and gagged
and grabbed
the side of the stage.

35

Luther sank to the floor.
His body curled into a ball.
Then it sprang straight
as a pine board.
"Arrrrrg!" he yelled again.
He rolled onto his back
and shot both legs
into the air.

Just as he was getting
to the best part,
Dr. Miracle said,
"That's enough, boy!"

The people screamed and hollered,
"Do something!
Help the boy, Dr. Miracle!"

Luther opened one eye a little.

He saw Miss Primm trembling.

He could not see his mother.

He guessed she had passed out.

He gave his legs
one last shake.

Dr. Miracle held up his hand.
"Don't worry, folks.

Dr. Miracle will save him."
He bent down beside Luther
and popped the top
off the bottle.

Luther's nose twitched.

The bottle smelled

like week-old creek water.

Dr. Miracle poured some

into Luther's mouth.

"Get up, boy," he whispered.

"Show them you're alive and well."

Luther got to his feet.
The crowd clapped.
Some people moved forward.
"One dime will buy you
health and happiness!"
Dr. Miracle shouted.

The sheriff walked
toward the wagon.
Dr. Miracle watched him.
The people pressed coins
into Dr. Miracle's hands.
He pushed bottles back at them.

Beneath Luther's shirt
the toad wiggled.
Luther giggled.
Rrrrrrroark! the toad croaked.
"Keep that thing quiet, boy,"
Dr. Miracle snapped.

43

Just then the toad leaped free.
It jumped
onto Miss Primm's nose.
Then it leaped into the dark,
screaming, *Rrrrrrroark!*
"Fake," someone shouted.
Soon everyone was calling,
"Fake! Fake! Fake!"

The sheriff was ever so close.
"Unhitch the horses, boy,"
Dr. Miracle whispered to Luther.

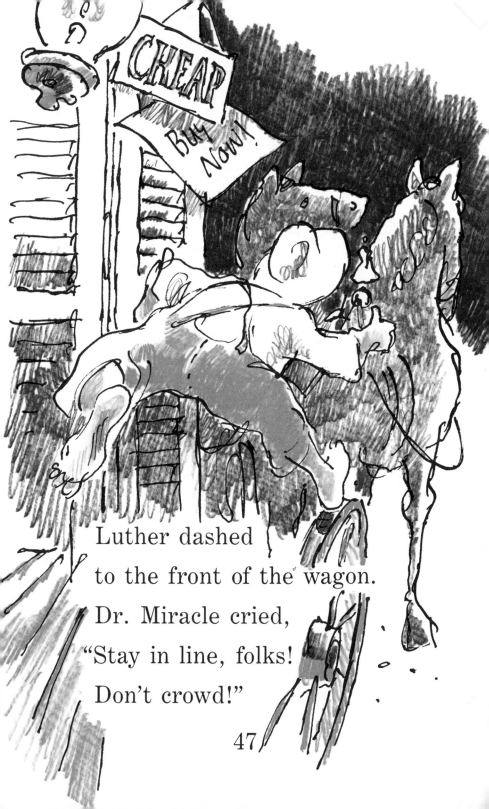

Luther dashed
to the front of the wagon.
Dr. Miracle cried,
"Stay in line, folks!
Don't crowd!"

47

The sheriff
reached the wagon.
Dr. Miracle smiled.
He shouted,
"You will all get your money back.
Don't shove, folks!"

48

Quickly Dr. Miracle
sprang into action.
He leaped
to the front of the wagon.
He grabbed the horses' reins.
"Giddap!" he yelled.

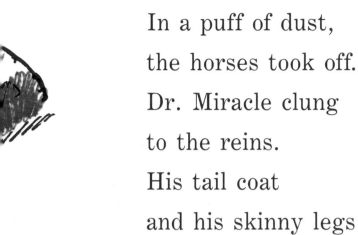

In a puff of dust,
the horses took off.
Dr. Miracle clung
to the reins.
His tail coat
and his skinny legs
flew up and down.

But the wagon still sat
right where it had been.
Bottles and dimes
were scattered over its stage.

Luther grinned.
"He wanted me
to unhitch the horses
from the post
so he could get away,"
Luther told the crowd.
"But I unhitched them
from the wagon, too!"

The sheriff laughed.
"You sure did, Luther!"
Luther's grin spread
clear across his face.
"Leave it to
a *dumb* kid like me
to mess things up!"

Miss Primm could not
stop fanning herself.
She said, "Why, Luther!
I would say
that was right *smart* of you."

55

The people picked up their dimes.
The cloud of dust settled.
In the shadows a toad croaked.
Rrrrrrroark!